CHILL CHOMP CHILL!

by **Chris Ayala-Kronos**

illustrated by **Paco Sordo**

Houghton Mifflin Harcourt

Boston   New York

DOWNLOAD
CHOMP'S SONG AT

HMHBOOKS.COM/
FREEDOWNLOADS

WITH THE CODE
CHILLCHOMP

Chomp loves playtime at school—especially when he gets to build with colorful blocks.

Chomp only needs one more purple block to complete his colorful castle. But just as he reaches for it . . .

Camara takes the very last purple block!
Oh no! What should Chomp do?

Every cubby has an invitation
to Rio's birthday party . . .

. . . except for Chomp's!

Chomp starts to worry.
What should Chomp do?

Should Chomp

FROWN?

Should Chomp

CRY?

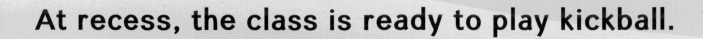

At recess, the class is ready to play kickball.

KICK!

Rio is up . . .
and boots a monster-big ball . . .

right toward Chomp!

Chomp makes the catch!

But everyone doesn't look as happy as he thought they'd be . . .

What should Chomp do?

Thanks for fixing our ball, Chomp!

After recess, the class is in for a great surprise . . .

Chomp was the first one back to class . . .
all alone with the buttery, delicious snack . . .

His mouth starts to water . . .
Then his tummy growls . . .
What should Chomp do?

Yum! Some times are just right for **chomping!**

To my dad, Tom, for being THE chillest —C.A.-K.

For Ainhoa, thank you for always helping me chill —P.S.

hmhbooks.com

The illustrations in this book were created digitally.
The text type was set in Amescote Heavy.
The display type was hand-lettered.
Design by Phil Caminiti

Library of Congress Cataloging-in-Publication Data is on file.

ISBN 978-0-358-41098-0

Manufactured in China
SCP 10 9 8 7 6 5 4 3 2 1
4500822894